Cookie Rescue

By Susan Ring
Illustrated by Alan Batson

DISNEP
PRESS

NEW YORK

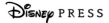

First Edition
Library of Congress Cataloging-in-Publication Data on file
ISBN-13: 978-1-4231-1026-2
ISBN-10: 1-4231-1026-9

Manufactured in the USA
For more Disney Press fun, visit www.disneybooks.com

The  is out in Sheet Rock Hills.

sun

Manny takes the tools for a ride.

Manny

Look! Here comes Mrs. Portillo.
She runs over to the .
truck
Maybe she has some of her
yummy .
cookies

"I don't smell any  ," says  .

cookies

Dusty

Mrs. Portillo can't bake cookies for

the town's Best Baker contest.

She needs help with her new  .

oven

Manny

and the tools will help.
They will move her new oven
into her **house**.
*Uno...dos...tres...cuatro...cinco
...seis...siete...*
Let's get to work!

Oh, no! The oven does not fit.

It is too big for the .
door

How will Mrs. Portillo

bake  for
cookies

the contest?

"I will tap it in," says .
Pat

"I will cut the door," says .
Dusty

No, no. That won't work!

Here comes Mr. Lopart and

Fluffy

Fluffy really wants to say hello!

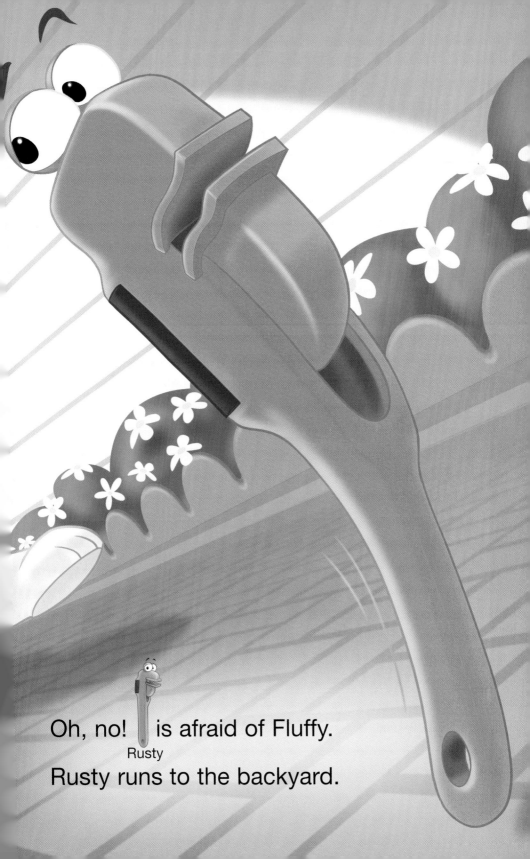

Oh, no! is afraid of Fluffy.

Rusty

Rusty runs to the backyard.

Thump!

Rusty runs into the back .

Fluffy makes sure that Rusty is okay.

door

has a good idea!

Stretch

They will take down the big .

door

The oven will fit now.

The new  is in the house.
oven

Mrs. Portillo can bake her  !
cookies

Here comes .
Mrs. Portillo

Does she need more help?

No. She has ![cookies] for everyone!
cookies

Yummy!